MOONBOY

Written and Illustrated by

Carolyn Garcia

BEYOND
WORDS
Publishing
I N C

Beyond Words Publishing, Inc.

20827 N.W. Cornell Road, Suite 500
Hillsboro, Oregon 97124-9808
503-531-8700 / 1-800-284-9673

Edited by Marianne Monson-Burton and Michelle Roehm
Designed by Amy A. B. Collen
Proofread by Heath Silberfeld

Distributed to the book trade by Publishers Group West
Printed & Bound by Ajanta Offset, India

The corporate mission of Beyond Words Publishing, Inc: Inspire To Integrity

Library of Congress Cataloging-in-Publication Data

Garcia, Carolyn.
       Moonboy / written and illustrated by Carolyn Garcia.
          p.   cm.
       Summary: The son of the Man in the Moon has no one to play with, so he goes down to earth to make some friends.
       ISBN 1-885223-81-1 (cloth)
       [1. Moon--Fiction. 2. Friendship--Fiction.] I. Title.
PZ7.G15562Mo   1999
[E]--dc21   98-41584
                                                     CIP
                                                       AC

For

Ann, Tanislado, and Johnathan Garcia.
Also for Jay, Sharon, Ray, Zola, Lorenzo, and Aiden.

Special thanks to

Stephen Kurowski

Moonboy was inspired by my dear friend
Alison O'Donoghue's wonderful sculpture which she called Moonboy.
"Could you write a story about Moonboy for my daughter Zola?" she asked.
I said "Yes," and that's how this book began.

Moonboy gazed through the swirling, twinkling night sky at Earth. "Will you take me there, Father?" Moonboy asked, shivering with excitement.

"You know my work is never done. I have to pull the tides in all the oceans on Earth," said the Old Man in the Moon, his face grinning with pride. Then the Old Man paused, the smile on his face fading. "I knew the day would come when you would want to see new things."

"I don't want to leave you," Moonboy said, "but I do wish I could go there."

Suddenly Moonboy felt light as dust. As he floated away his father called, "You won't be alone. I will shine down on you, my sweet boy, and please shine back at me."

On
a
swish
of
a
wish,
Moonboy
flew
toward
Earth.

He landed atop a hill
overlooking the town
of Poppygold.

Moonboy clapped his hands when he saw the people of the town coming and going. He noticed a boy doing cartwheels across a green lawn. "Hello!" the people said to one another. "How are you? Nice weather we're having!"

Moonboy ran down the hill toward a group of children.

"Hello Hello Hello!"

he sang, turning three cartwheels. The children stared at him with their mouths hanging open. They looked at each other and ran away. *Did I do something wrong?* Moonboy wondered.

He walked into town, turning cartwheels and saying "Hello!" to every person he saw, but the people didn't say a thing. They only looked at him out of narrowed eyes and hurried away, whispering to each other.

Moonboy returned to the hilltop and watched
as the people disappeared into their houses.
He decided that he should have one, too. In a wish,
there was his house. It was different from the
houses of Poppygold, but Moonboy liked
it very much. Now that he had a house,
he went outside every morning and waited
for people to come and say hello.

"Nice weather we're having," he practiced
saying, even when it rained.

But no one came to see him.
Instead, they pointed at his house
and rushed away when he
waved to them.

Is my house wrong?
he thought sadly.

One night he tiptoed through
town and peeked inside the
houses. In one house the people
were having a party. He heard them singing
"Happy birthday to you!" A smile rose on Moonboy's
face. *A party!* he thought. *I'll have a birthday
party and invite them all. Then they will
say, "Hello!"*

Back at his own house, Moonboy wished
for a table and chairs. He wished for lots
of food and a birthday cake with blazing candles.
All night he stayed up making party hats, confetti,
and decorations.

Early the next morning he crept down into Poppygold
and delivered his invitations. Moonboy rushed back
up the hill and put on a party hat.

He was so excited that he glowed brightly and
thought, *I hope my father can see me now!*

Moonboy waited. And waited.

Whenever someone came near the hill,
he sprang to his feet, cartwheeled, and
yelled, "Nice weather we're having!" But nobody
answered. Nobody came.

Moonboy sat alone at his table. Sadly he sang,
"Happy birthday to youuuu. . . ." Then he squinched
his eyes and wished for a friend, but nothing
happened.

"I wish for a friend!" he cried.

He looked around hopefully,
but no one appeared.

In Poppygold, Ed Bread stood in his room, gazing at Moonboy's house. Ed held the invitation Moonboy had delivered to his doorstep. He had wanted to go to the party, but everyone had said, "We mustn't go. We dare not go! That new boy's head glows!"

Ed didn't understand what they meant, so he decided to find out.

The following day, Ed went to Cee Cee Shiny's house. Her daughters, Bee and Truly, met him at the door and chimed, "Wipe your shoes on the mat, Ed!"

"Sit on this towel!" Truly said, before Ed could settle onto the gleaming white couch.

Ed sat stiffly but came right to the point. "Why do people think the new boy is weird?"

"Because he has two odd little doors where his shirt should be!" Truly shrieked.

Cee Cee hissed, "What's behind those doors on his chest? That's what I want to know." She leaned close to Ed, spraying a cloud of air freshener above his head.

"I think he's full of dust bunnies" she confided

"And dust chickens and dust dogs,"
Truly squealed.

"Dogs that SHED!" Bee joined in with furious glee.
"Dust rhinos! Dust hippopotami! Dust elephants!"

"Spots and dust," shuddered Cee Cee. "Yes, yes.
If we'd gone to that party our dresses would have
gotten gray and greasy!"

$\mathcal{N}$ext Ed visited the baker, Leroy Sprinkle. Leroy was rolling out pie dough and squinting at Moonboy's house through a telescope. "I see you're looking at the new boy's house. What do *you* think of him?" Ed asked politely.

In dreadful tones Leroy Sprinkle said, "There's a *machine* inside of him. A super souped-up, cooking-making, doughnut-shaping, pie-baking machine!" He let out a sob. "That machine in his chest will put me out of business! His party was just an excuse for people to sample his machine-made pies— lemon meringue, chocolate, coconut cream!"

When Ed said good-bye, Leroy didn't answer. He was too busy peering through the telescope and rolling his pie dough to pieces.

Across the street Slim and Ezma Biddle lived in a horribly hot house filled with cactus plants. When Ed asked them about the new boy, Ezma began to shiver. "Slim and I know what's behind those doors of his. Ice-cold shivery rivery murky blue water." Ezma's false teeth chattered.

Slim grabbed a blanket and wrapped it around his shoulders. "Cold water!" he agreed. "Full of slimy squids and electric eels and a giant octopus that'll shoot icy ink in yer eye. He woulda opened those doors at that party and flooded us right offa that hill."

"Some party," Ezma sniffled. "Stay away from him or he'll turn you into a snowman. **Brrrrr!**"

Ed nodded, but now he knew. There was only one way to find out about Moonboy. He would have to see for himself.

Up the hill Ed went, trying not to be scared. Moonboy saw him coming and called, "Hello! Hello! Nice weather we're having!"

"Uh . . . hello," Ed stammered. He wanted to run away, but he made himself stand still.

"I'm Moonboy!" The new boy smiled and his head glowed like a hundred fireflies. "Want to see my house? Want to have a party?"

"Uh, maybe," said Ed. Then he forgot his manners and blurted, "Everyone thinks you're weird. They think you have bad stuff behind those doors. What's *inside* of you, Moonboy?"

"What's inside of YOU?" asked Moonboy, pointing at Ed's chest.

"Just bones and a heart," Ed answered, trying to remember science lessons.

"But what's _in_ your heart?" Moonboy asked.

Suddenly Ed understood exactly what Moonboy meant. In a rush he said, "Mom and Dad and my brothers and sisters. My goldfish in her bowl. Sand at the beach. My red bike. Lots of neat things."

"Me, too," said Moonboy, while reaching for the glass knobs on his front. Ed held his breath, and slowly Moonboy's doors began to open . . .

"Now will you be my friend?" asked Moonboy.

"YES!" shouted Ed as he turned a cartwheel. Moonboy cartwheeled, too. Upside down they grinned at each other. "Let's go show everyone in Poppygold what's in you!" Ed hollered.

"Do you think they'll come here for a party?" asked Moonboy.

"Let's find out!" Ed replied. He rolled down the hill with Moonboy right behind him. Ed took hold of Moonboy's hand and together they showed everyone in Poppygold who Moonboy *really* was.

Together they prepared for the party, and when they saw the people of Poppygold coming up the hill, they opened the door wide and yelled,

"Helloooo!"